Chapter

I stepped out of the shower, dried off, and threw my hair up into a towel. I grabbed my body moisturizer and began lathering up my body. As I massaged up toward my belly and then my breasts I caught a glance at myself in the mirror. I stopped what I was doing and turned to face myself. I stared at my reflection, admiring the female form. I hadn't always loved my reflection but with the hard work I had been putting in at the gym, it was finally starting to show. Before I could finish looking myself over I was startled by the bathroom door handle rattling.

"Hey Ab, are you out of the shower?" My Boyfriend, Mike, yelled.

I quickly got up, put the mirror away, and headed out of the bathroom.

"Ya, it's all yours if you want it," I replied as I walked into the bedroom. He was back sitting on the bed watching the TV.

"No I don't need the bathroom, I was just wondering why it was taking you so long," He replied without lifting his eyes from the TV. I rolled my eyes and put my pajamas on.

"What? I can't have a two-hour-long shower?" I joked knowing I hadn't taken more than 20 minutes.

He didn't reply and kept staring at the TV. I slid my nightgown on hoping he wouldn't glance at my naked body. I knew if he caught sight of me changing he would think he's entitled to my body somehow. Thankfully he was too interested in the hockey documentary he was watching, to look anywhere else. I laid down, picked up my novel, and started reading.

My eyes grew heavy within minutes and I decided to put down the book and close my eyes. Within seconds Mike must have picked up that I was ready to fall asleep because he turned the TV off and cuddled up next to me. Pressing his hard member against me, I felt his hands wrap around me as he reached under my nightie. I wasn't really in the mood but I knew I'd hear about it in the morning if I turned him down. He wasn't violent or anything, but Mike has always been insecure and needy in our relationship, and with a high sex drive it causes some major insecurities sometimes. If I said no to intimacy he took it to heart, even though we do it every second night, he will think something is wrong.

I lifted my nightie and wriggled my butt next to his naked dick. I felt the soft tip of his penis push against my pussy. He grabbed my hips and positioned himself closer as I felt him enter me. I felt him hard and deep as he grabbed my hair pulling my head close to him. My back arched as he held himself inside me.

"I knew you wanted it, you can't resist me can you?" His breath was heavy as he pulled out and thrust back into me as hard. I had to admit it did feel good but I always felt something was missing in our sex life.

He let go of my hair to put both hands on my hips and began to thrust hard and quickly into me. A few seconds later he stopped.

"You want to get on top?" he asked between thrusts.

"I'm really tired, and this feels good anyway," I replied.

"Ok, I'll get on top," He pulled me to lay on my back and I spread my legs.

I felt him push into me again, this time pushing deeper. I could feel he was more erect now. He pulled out and pushed back in slowly and then pushed deep into me where he held it. Seconds later I felt him throbbing inside me, his warm cum filling me.

He rolled over and lay silently. I waddled to the toilet to clean up. Minutes later, I climbed back into bed to him fast asleep.

Tossing and turning that night, I couldn't help but have thoughts about a woman's hand touching my body and caressing my breasts. I felt the ache between my legs and reached down, fantasizing my hand was someone else's hand. I played with my clit gently. envisioning a woman opening her legs and envisioning I was touching her. I then envisioned a woman touching me, massaging my pussy and gently fingering me. Quickly, I brought myself to orgasm, grabbing the pillow to stifle my moans.

* * *

When I was done, I opened my eyes and felt the silence in the room, no more snoring next to me.

Did I wake him? I thought.

I tried not to move a muscle and held my breath trying to figure out if he would say something. I had never been caught masturbating and I knew it was risky to do it beside him but I had done it a million times before without him ever waking. Suddenly a loud snore came tumbling out of him and I sighed with relief.

The next morning I awoke to the sunlight coming in through the blinds. I rolled over and noticed I was alone. My watch read 7:19 am. I rubbed my eyes and sat up, hearing a click from the front door. Confused, I got up and walked through the apartment.

"Mike?" I called out. No answer.

I went back to the bedroom and grabbed my phone off the nightstand. I sent Mike a text, asking why he had left early. I knew he wasn't expected at the office until 9 am.

My phone rang a minute later.

"Hello?" I answered anxiously.

"Hey Ab," Mike answered, I could hear he was in the car. "Sorry, I left early I wanted to get a jump start on some of these new projects coming in. I didn't think I would wake you,".

"Oh,"' I said disappointed. He's been leaving early every day this week.

"Ya, sorry hun, I should have told you. How was your sleep? Did you just get up?"

"Ya, um it was good thanks, how was yours?"

"Great, anyway I'm heading into the city now I'll talk to you later," he hung up before I could say anything more. I stared at the phone for a second thinking maybe he would call back, but I knew I wouldn't hear from him until later that night. It's been busy for Mike and I try to respect his space but sometimes I felt like something was missing in all of this. We used to text each other all day or video call on lunch breaks, but now I felt like I was alone and just going through the motions of life, not living it. I dreaded the next step in a relationship, Marriage, or worse, kids. I felt like there wasn't anything fun to look forward to anymore.

I made a coffee and opened up my laptop at the kitchen table. I checked my emails and found mostly junk mail, so I decided to browse the job boards. We had moved here just over four months ago and I still hadn't found work. I know Mike said he would take care of me until I found something, but I hated feeling dependent on someone. I left my job back home so Mike could pursue his career full-time here. It was hard not to feel a little resentful when things were working out so well for him and I sat at home alone, unable to secure a job interview. City life is a lot more competitive than I had thought.

However there was one benefit to moving, I got to hang out with my best friend Sarah more. Sarah's always had a busy schedule, but as long as she wasn't out of town for her job, the two of us had been hanging out every weekend. She knew all the hot spots and the hidden gems in the city, from the bars to nightclubs, and coffee shops to late-night diners.

I checked the calendar and realized Sarah would be away for a convention this weekend. I sighed and thought about what I would do with all this free time. Fridays, Mike insists on watching the hockey game together, it's 'our night' he says but picks everything from the game to the food to the drink. Saturdays are what he calls 'Guys Day' aka a regular boys' night but it's all day *and* night. He is always so preoccupied, never any time to enjoy city life with me. I needed to find something exciting to do on the weekends.

Chapter 2

Most of the next few days were spent hanging out at coffee shops or applying for jobs, still trying to come up with something to do for the weekend. I finally decided to try out a new hobby, painting. It was something that would kill a few hours and I might even like the final product enough to hang it on our bare walls. I spent the rest of the week gathering supplies and deciding on the picture to paint. By Thursday I had watched hours of how-to-paint videos and felt excited to start the scenic picture I had chosen.

That Thursday night I fell asleep before Mike even made it home from work. He had been working late at night on some fancy project. I found it annoying how he would never fill me in on things or leave everything open-ended so I never knew when to expect him. I also understood he probably didn't know when things would be done or maybe he was too tired to come home and talk about work. I didn't know, but it sure wasn't like this at the beginning of our relationship. He was excited to fill me in on every little detail of his life in the beginning. I guess being together for so long things start to wear off.

The dream I had that night was one I will never forget. It was so vivid it felt real. There was a woman, and she was slowly dancing toward me. I am not sure where we were but we were sitting on pillows surrounded by silk. There was a bright light behind her so I couldn't make out any details at first. The outline of her silhouette became more and more defined as she approached. I could see her hips, the roundness in her bum, and as she turned, I could see the shape of her breasts, full and round with pointy nipples. She leaned toward me and I could see her face through a sheer black veil. She removed the veil slowly pushing it over her head and began trying to say something to me. Her mouth was moving, her burgundy colored lipstick capturing my attention but I couldn't hear anything she was saying. Closer and closer she approached me and my heart began to race. Refusing to take my eyes off her, not even to blink, she was mesmerizing. She got so close I could smell her, I had never smelled in a dream before. She smelled like sweet flowers and her skin was covered in sparkles. I could see she was naked and it instantly turned me on, feeling excited for the first time in a long time. I realized I was naked, but before I could do anything about it, the woman leaned down and gently lifted my chin. Looking me deep in the eyes, her gaze playful as her green eyes looked right through me. With her mesmerizing stare, she gently brushed my lips with her finger. I could tell she knew what I wanted. She bit her lip and her eyes slowly looked down at my lips. Her gaze glossed over as she leaned in further, my thighs clenching together as I could feel the heat between my legs rising. I was aching for something, I needed it, whatever it was she had it. I wanted her, to kiss me, to touch me. I leaned into her and our lips softly brushed each other. We held it there for half a second and I pushed in further, kissing her with hunger. As we kissed, I could feel her hand on my thigh, slowly going up. Her lips on mine still, I spread my legs yearning for her touch, I felt myself getting wet. I felt her hand between my legs gently touching me. I ached for her, expecting her fingers to have plunged inside me, but instead, I felt emptiness.

I opened my eyes and stared up at the popcorn ceiling in our apartment. The fan was blowing but I was still sweating. I blinked a few times trying to understand what happened, *did I dream that?* It made sense in my dream, but as I woke up I realized I had no idea who that woman was or why that happened. I felt between my legs and sure enough, I was soaked, completely drenched.

I looked at my calendar, it was January 4th. I opened my phone and went to my period app, January 4 would mean it is, Ovulation Day, *of course.* My hormones must be going wild and I'm dreaming up crazy situations. I stopped the pill two months ago so that Mike and I can begin trying to conceive. It's been something I have been debating for a long time, being 34 now and my husband being 37 we had to make a decision. He has always wanted a big family, he comes from a big family and so I agreed. Deep down, I still didn't know if I even wanted kids or to get pregnant. I enjoyed our sex life for the last 8 years together when we weren't trying to get pregnant. It wasn't perfect, but this makes me not want to have sex at all.

I sent him a text about it being ovulation day and decided to go take a shower. I closed my eyes as I leaned under the hot water and suddenly the same woman from my dream was back in my mind. I smiled, kept my eyes closed, and decided to see where this went.

She was dancing again, slowly and sultry-like. She smiled and walked over to me, I could see she was completely naked. Her breasts swayed as she walked, and I wanted to reach out and touch them. Her long shiny black hair draped around her like a silk shawl. I thought about her touching my body as I began to massage my breasts in the shower. I envisioned her kissing my nipples as I gently played with mine, rubbing the tips between my fingers. I wanted to feel hers in my mouth, I wanted her breasts on my face, her lips on mine. The shower was getting hot but I could feel the warmth between my legs more. I envisioned her putting her hand down my belly, slowly reaching down to my pubic area. I gasped as I envisioned her hand reaching past my pubic hair and gently caressing my clit. I could feel the throbbing in me as I yearned for more pressure. She smiled at me as she reached farther between my legs, I opened up as she slowly reached a finger inside me, warm, wet, and ready. Using one finger she gently played with my clit and with perfect pressure I couldn't escape. She put two fingers inside me as she hit all the right spots. I felt the build-up of an orgasm, I was ready and in my mind, she was the one to do it for me. Just as I was about to let go I heard the bathroom door open.

Chapter 3

Mike walked into the bathroom to brush his teeth. I held my breath and held my pussy hoping I wouldn't cum. He seemed to be taking his time and my orgasm was disappearing with every second. Annoyed, I decided to just finish washing up and get out.

"I didn't know you were home," I said to him as I grabbed a towel.

"I took the day off, I worked too much last night. Sorry, I was at the condo gym I figured I'd let you sleep in. Done with the shower?" He asked.

"Um, ya. You could have jumped in with me. I don't know if you read my text..." referring to the ovulation text I sent.

"Oh, yes. I did sorry I was just busy at the time. Um, ya we will definitely get on that tonight." He didn't sound very excited but could be because he is exhausted.

"We don't have to, you know," I say as he pauses getting into the shower.

"Well, maybe you're right," he seemed to agree. "I'm

just tired," he said as he got in the shower. I felt mixed emotions like something was bothering him.

I walked away wondering what that meant. He was the one who was pressuring us to be parents. It could be the move, he might want to wait until he's not so busy with work. I just found it odd he changed his mind so soon. Especially after how many years of talking about having a big family together.

Later that day Mike came home and we had our usual Friday night pizza and drinks, while we watched the hockey game on the TV. I wasn't much for drinking, especially with trying to conceive in the near future, but Mike insisted we 'relax' on Fridays. I also didn't care for Hockey but it was the only sport I would agree to watch because I understood it.

"So basically Dave says the trip will be free, and I'll be reimbursed for any extra expense, I mean, what do you think Ab?" He asked while taking a bite from his pizza. Mike was going on about his upcoming business trip to Hawaii. It confused me that they needed to go to Hawaii of all places but as Mike liked to point out I 'didn't understand the business' so I mostly just nod and agree. All I could think about was some free time with nothing to do, again. At this rate, I will have plenty of new hobbies mastered.

We finished our drinks as the clock ran out in the game. I grabbed the dishes from the living room and tidied up the kitchen. Mike went to the downstairs bathroom while I washed my face in the master bath. I put my nightie on and lay in bed waiting for him. I contemplated pretending to be asleep but he walked in before I could make a decision.

"So?" he looked at me with that look.

"So what?" I ask rolling over, pretending to yawn.

"Do you want to?"

I rolled back over. *Where did the romance go?* I wondered.

"Want to what?" I sighed.

I felt him crawl into bed next to me.

"We don't have to make a baby, ill pull out tonight,". I felt him push against me. I turned around and grabbed his dick in my hand and began to massage it as he grew harder and harder.

"Just a handy," I whispered.

When he had finished and fallen asleep, I was wide awake beside him. He began to snore and I quietly got up to tip-toe into the kitchen to make a sleep tea.

As I filled up the kettle I could hear a vibration come from a coat pocket.

Did I forget my phone in my jacket again? I

wondered.

I turned the kettle on and walked over to the coats. In the dark, I reached into the pockets of my jacket, but there was no phone. I figured I must have been hearing things but as I walk away the buzz goes off again. I turned back around thinking maybe he forgot his phone. I know he needs his alarm in the morning so I reached into his coat pocket. Sure enough, his phone was in there. I pulled it out to bring it to his bedside table, but as I glance at the phone I stop in my tracks.

A text across the screen read:

T-minus 7 days!! Can't wait to be naked in Hawaii with you Mikey! xoxo
Sent from a woman named Kendra.

Mikey? I thought, confused. *And who is Kendra?*

I opened up the message. My heart sank further and further into the pit of my stomach. Text upon texts of constant flirting and steamy pictures. Some nude pictures, some of them together, naked at the office, in their cars, and at some point they went golfing together. They also have pictures of the two of them at the restaurant. I felt the emotions rise in my throat. I had seen enough and decided to screen-capture some evidence and send it to my phone. Once I had done that I crawled back into bed and laid awake, silently crying, until he got up for work.

Around 7:30 the next morning I heard the click of

the front door and I got straight up to begin packing. I may have cried it out all night but I also had a lot of time to think. He and I shouldn't be together, we're two different people. I am miserable, he is *clearly* miserable and seeking enjoyment elsewhere. I don't know why I hadn't seen this before but we should never have been together. I went for the easy route, settle with a guy, get married, have kids, etc. I didn't realize it when I was younger but I was not meant for this mediocre life, especially if I'm going to bed dealing with side chicks all the time I can't trust him anyway. I decided on leaving that day before he got home. I was going to start living only for me. I thought about how I didn't even want kids yet felt pressured by him, what a bullet I dodged. I wrote out a lengthy note, left copies of their steamy texts, and left. I just needed to figure out where I was going.

After some thought, I called up the furthest hotel from his condo and booked a room. It wasn't fancy by any means, just a bed, dresser, a small TV, and a green upholstered chair in the corner. It smelled of stale cigarettes and cleaning products. I walked over to the blackout curtains and opened them all the way up letting in a thick beam of light, highlighting the dust floating around the room. I unpacked what I brought with me and considered going down to the bar for a drink but decided to text my bestie first. I knew she was out of town so I didn't think I would get a quick response but to my surprise, she replied within minutes.

Chapter 4

'Hey, girl! I miss you too! I'll call you when I get a min.' her text read. I decided to try to occupy myself in the hotel room until then. There wasn't much else to do but unpack and make the place mine for a while.

After an hour of mulling about in the stale hotel room, I decided to open up my laptop and redo my resume in hopes to get any job at this point. Scrolling through emails I noticed a pop-up ad in the corner of the screen.

'Hot singles near you!' It read.

I laughed, trying to click the x on the corner of the screen. Instead, I accidentally clicked on the link. It redirected me to a website full of naked women. I don't know what came over me but I had to stop and look. I scrolled up and down the page feeding my curiosity until I stumbled on a gorgeous brunette woman's profile.

'New to Girls' it read. *Same,* I thought jokingly.

I couldn't help myself so I clicked on the link. She was naked and her legs spread wide open, instantly exciting me. She was beautiful and for some reason, I couldn't help but imagine kissing her entire body. From her beautiful lips to her tiny pink nipples, down her belly, and in between. At this point, I wanted to see more so I clicked on the video and began to watch.

She was mesmerizing, so soft and sultry. My whole body began to tingle, my nipples becoming hard as I felt myself getting turned on. I felt my breasts and began to massage and rub my nipples. It felt wrong but so right at the same time.

I felt the heat building between my legs, spreading them apart I could feel the wetness leak into my underwear. Reaching one hand down my pants to feel, I watched in awe as the woman on the screen was met with another beautiful naked woman. I could tell this girl was nervous. My clit was throbbing as they kissed and massaged each other's breasts, one of them now sitting on the other. It was incredibly hot to watch as her pussy was spread open. I watched her fingers go into the other girl. I couldn't take my eyes away as I began to rub vigorously between my legs, feeling my clit stiffen between my fingers as I applied more and more pressure. I could hear the juices coming out of the girl being fingered, and suddenly a splash onto the other girl's lap. She seemed almost embarrassed, but then they both gave a little giggle while she began licking up her cum off the other girl's legs. I could feel myself building up an orgasm as I watched. Her tongue dripped with the clear slippery fluid, I wanted to taste it more than anything.

Then, without warning, the girl licking up her cum spread the other girls' legs far apart exposing her pussy and ass. I had to slow myself down so I could watch what happened as I was right on the edge, feeling more and more liquid slipping between my fingers into my underwear. Her tongue circled the girl's clit and then slid in and out of her. She inserted a finger and I could see she was feeling for the gspot. My pussy throbbed between my fingers, ready for release. I watched as the bottom girl began to uncontrollably squirt and orgasm. I pressed my fingers into my pussy and felt my swollen gspot. Stroking it once with my finger, I felt a sudden gush run past my hands and the waves of an orgasm strongly flowing through me. I cried out as I felt more liquid release as my pussy contracted.

The waves of euphoria tapered off and I sunk into the chair. Breathing heavily, I looked at my pants and notice the large wet spot, something I had never done before. I had always been wet when I orgasmed but never that much, soaking my pants through to the chair. Thinking about it, I hadn't experienced that strong of an orgasm in a long time, a few years at least. I never realized how unhappy I was in my relationship, maybe I needed adventure and this was my body's way of saying it. I had always been into men, but what I just witnessed was something entirely different and it felt new and exciting.

I decided to take a shower and clean up. As I got into the shower, I couldn't help but feel bad. Had I done something wrong? Why did I feel like I had done something wrong? I'm not in a relationship anymore, but why did that feel so wrong? I began washing my body as tears slowly streamed down my face alongside the water. I felt confused, was I crying for Mike? Was I crying because I felt horrible about the breakup? Was I crying because for once I finally found something that made me feel something? I couldn't put my finger on it. I turned the shower off, grabbed my towel, and sank to the bottom of the tub to cry into my knees. Then, without warning, my phone rang.

* * *

Chapter 5

It was my Bestie, Sarah.

"Girl what's going on?" she asked with concern.

"Mike and I broke up, we're done. He's cheating and I didn't even say goodbye" I started to ball, tears streaming down my face.

"Oh girl, I am so sorry to hear this! I knew something was wrong, you never text me when I am out of town. I can't believe Mike!" She said in disbelief.

"I know, I felt like things have been off for a while," I remind her.

"Yea, but every relationship has its ups and downs. I didn't think it was this bad, so he's like for real cheating? Like, did you catch him?"

"It's all there in the texts, pictures of them, they have little love names for each other," I cried. "How could he do this? I even agreed to have kids and I should have known when he began to beat around the bush when I quit the pill. I should have known he never took us seriously, 8 long years I've wasted. I'm basically a spinster now!"

* * *

"What's wrong with being a spinster?" She laughed trying to cheer me up, reminding me that she hadn't had a solid relationship in years.

"Right," I sniffed and smiled. "I guess I can just join you in your lifestyle now. Honestly, I don't feel that upset about leaving, I thought about it all night and we were never right for each other. We were forcing things because we had been together for so long and we were comfortable. He's an incredibly selfish person and I just need to be my own person now. Live the single life," I sighed feeling a weight off my chest.

"That is so true! As long as I have known you, you've been with Mike! This will be all new for you and we will have fun I promise! I'm booking a return flight home for tomorrow morning," She said as I heard her put me on speaker.

"No, don't come home for me," I protested. "I'll be fine until you're done with your trip,".

"No, I am. I want to, I don't know why you're the one staying in a hotel, it should be him, but you are not alone. I will be back tomorrow and you can stay with me in my condo." I could hear her nails clicking on the phone while she typed.

"You're sure about this?" I asked.

"Yes, we both don't have families to fall back on, we need each other! I know you would do the same for me.

I will be there tomorrow by 10:35 am can you pick me up from the airport?"

"Of course," I sniff, slowly drying the tears from my face. She was right, we had mutually bonded in college over the fact we had lost our moms in early childhood.

"OK, I'm going to wrap this stuff up and I'm coming home! Take care of yourself and don't do anything crazy until I get there" she said.

As we hung up I couldn't help but smile and feel the warmth of having a good friend in my life. What would I do without her? Besides, I was excited that we can get together more.

Just as I dozed off to sleep, my phone rang again. It was Mike's number. I let it go to voice mail and then checked the message.

"Look, I am sorry. I know I messed up, I really messed up. I just want to be honest with you, will you call me back so we can talk?"

My heart broke listening to his voice. I called him and we spent over an hour on the phone talking openly about what had happened. He admitted to cheating and falling out of love with me, he was in love with Kendra and didn't know how to break it to me. I admitted I didn't want children and wasn't sure what I wanted anymore and we both agreed this was for the best. We split peacefully as difficult as it was.

* * *

The next day I was anxiously waiting at the terminal by 10:00 am. I felt nervous for some reason like I was meeting Sarah for the first time. An all-new me without the influence of Mike. I couldn't wait to experience life as a single girl with her best friend.

I paced around checking my watch every few minutes until I saw groups of people walking out of the terminal. My heart skipped a beat when I saw her. I felt time slow down as I saw her long shiny blond hair and bright smile walking toward me. I felt awkward, do we hug? Do we shake hands?

"Ab!!" She screamed and ran up to hug me, she smelled of sweet flowers it was so intoxicating. She melted all my awkward fears. I swear she is the only person who can take a 6-hour flight, change time zones and still come out looking and smelling amazing. We embraced for a few seconds and she released me looking me up and down. I blushed unexpectedly.

"You look amazing for someone experiencing heartache!" she laughed.

I smiled back at her.

"Thanks, it is so good to see you, you have no idea," I say feeling relieved and happy to see her. "Let me help you carry your things," I offer as we walk over to the conveyor belt.

We load up the luggage into my car and head to her condo downtown. The whole drive was spent on small talk, catching up about her trip and the amenities she stayed in.

We unloaded our suitcases and headed to the elevators to her penthouse condo. The elevator ride was long and I could tell Sarah was busy typing something out, probably working. I kept sneaking peeks at her and I couldn't help it, she just looked so good. I didn't even know why this was happening, we had known each other for years. I had never looked at her like this. I decided it is because I was going through a huge break-up and just needed to feel loved. That made the most sense, except for the glorious orgasm I had watching the two girls who looked like her, but I'm sure I can chalk that up to having not experienced a decent orgasm in years.

We unloaded the elevator and I followed her down the hall to her condo. Her place was covered with floor-to-ceiling windows with a beautiful view of the city's core. I've been here a million times and it's always as breathtaking as the last, especially at night.

She gave me the spare bedroom with the same windows and a private entrance to the balcony. I unpacked and put away my things while she got herself settled in.

"I'm just going to grab a shower," Sarah yelled from her room. I could hear her footsteps walking up the hall. She peeked her head into my room.

"And then, we can go for dinner and drinks!" She

squealed.

"Sure, any place in mind?" I smiled and turned around to face her, only to discover she was already naked. My eyes went wide and I dropped the shirt I was folding.

"What?" She asked surprised.

"Oh, um nothing I just...Was wondering where I should put my laptop," I tried hard not to make eye contact or look at her with my bright red face.

"Oh! Come with me, I'll show you,".

Still butt naked she led me into the living room where an empty desk sat. I tried not to look at her but it felt impossible.

"I have a spare desk, if you want to use it you're welcome to. My master bedroom has my work desk and everything I need so you can use this area," She explained.

I couldn't pay attention because I was just trying so hard not to stare at her perfect body. I started to get the urge to kiss her and began to imagine what her lips felt like. I kept my eyes on the desk until she walked back to the bathroom and started the shower. I noticed she hadn't shut the door and I didn't know what to do, my bedroom faced the bathroom. Should I go into my bedroom, close the door and unpack more or should I just hang out here until she's done? Why was I being so weird?

I decided to walk to my bedroom without looking into the bathroom though I desperately wanted to. As I turned into my bedroom I heard the shower curtain open up and Sarah was soaking wet leaning out of the shower.

"Hey Ab, can you grab me my purple shampoo for me? I completely forgot it's just under the sink in here" She pointed at the cabinet. I could see the water dripping off her nipples as she leaned over.

I walked over to the bathroom and grabbed her shampoo. She leaned out further to grab it exposing her belly. I gulped as I caught a glimpse of her before she disappeared behind the curtain.

I walked back to my room and sat on my bed staring at the bathroom. I could see the shadow of her behind the curtain, the outline of her perfect curves swaying as she washed up. I felt the heat building between my legs and decided to rub myself over my pants. I spread my legs and felt my underwear get wet, seeping through to my pants. Reaching into my pants I began to envision her without the shower curtain in the way. What she would look like soaked and naked sitting on my lap. I would play with her, feeling the inside of her soft velvety lips. Then watch her squirm as I hit the spot and make her cum all over me while her legs are spread on my lap.

I caressed my clit as I imagined we lay naked in

bed together. I thought about her kissing me everywhere, down my body, and between my legs. I used my fingers going in and out of me while I pictured it was her tongue or her fingers. I closed my eyes and began to moan as I felt the orgasm coming on, and just before it hit I heard the shower turn off and I pulled my hands out of my pants. I tried to stifle my orgasm but I still felt waves course through me, I let out an uncontrollable moan. Quickly I checked for any wet spots but thankfully I was wearing black pants.

* * *

Chapter 6

The cork popped off the sparkling bottle and Sarah poured us two glasses. As she passed my glass over, I couldn't help but take in her beauty. It was like I had just noticed her. Everything about her was holding me in a trance, even the perfume she chose was intoxicating.

"To our new life together! The Two of Us!" She laughed as we clinked glasses.

"Who needs men?" I laugh and take a sip. I felt the liquid hit my stomach with a warming feeling.

"Seriously, what kind of biological trick is it that we are even attracted to men?" She laughed. "Mind you, I have had relationships with women and sometimes they're not any better,".

"You have?" I asked, trying not to sound too excited.

"Oh, sure! Not recently, but in my early twenty's I had a girlfriend. I thought I truly loved her and you know what? That breakup was harder to get over than any other," She took a sip. "To be honest, she might be why I don't like commitment".

* * *

"That's awful, I'm so sorry," I replied.

"It's fine, that was over 10 years ago," She smiled and held her gaze for a moment. It felt like she could see through me, and read my thoughts. I felt exposed and didn't know what to say.

She walked over to the counter to grab a snack off the charcuterie board. She popped a piece of cheese in her mouth and opened up her phone. I realized I felt nervous and didn't know why, it had never happened before in her company.

"So we can go," she paused. "Apparently there is a DJ at the Rockstar Restaurant up the street, or we could go to Zemis. That place is always fun and happening," She continued looking through her phone.

I felt a twinge in my stomach, I wanted to stay here with her alone.

"Where ever," I say " We could even order in," I didn't want to sound too desperate.

"Order in? Girl, what? We need you to get back on the horse! We need to find sexy muscular dance partners with deep pockets" She winked.

"Oh no, that's fine. I'm not that upset with the break-up, Mike and I weren't on the same page for so many years now. I just needed to see it. Besides, we talked it out the other night, this was a long time coming,".

"Right, but you aren't going to stay celibate under my watch" She laughed. "Finish your drink, we need to go dancing. The city will be swimming with suits tonight,".

She walked over with the bottle and topped up my glass, then her own. She sat on the couch beside me and I could smell her sweet perfume again.

"You sure you don't want to stay here?" I didn't care if I sounded desperate.

"No way. We are not going to stay in here all night. I've been desperate to take you on the town with me and now that you're free we need to live this up!"

I caved and we finished our drinks before catching a cab downtown.

The restaurant was packed and somehow Sarah managed to get us past the line and the line without issue. We walked up to the first empty seats and a good-looking man made a beeline for us.

"Sarah!" The guy sang as he embraced her in a big hug. He had bleach blond hair slicked back. He reminded me of a modern-day Grease character.

"Phil!" She squealed back. "Phil this is my best

friend Abby, Abby this is Phil! He's the restaurant owner and we've known each other since that project I did in New York in 2016. He handled the whole event flawlessly and we just clicked,".

Phil scooped me up into a big hug as well. His cologne was strong and overpowering.

"So nice to meet you! I have a VIP room free for you two if you want. I can send a waiter up with a round of drinks for us." He turned around to wave down a waiter.

I followed the group up to the VIP room which was much more secluded and way quieter. The room was luxurious and inviting with plenty of velvet curtains and dim lighting. We took a seat and the waiter offered us drinks and appetizers as we chatted. Phil had to run to check on the other VIP rooms and Sarah and I were once again alone.

We sat in silence for a minute. My imagination ran wild picturing us making out all over this VIP room.

"Phil seems nice," I said trying to bring myself back to earth.

"Oh he is the best, but don't waste your time on him, he's gay" She replies bluntly.

"Oh, I wasn't, I didn't ..." I stumbled over my words. How do I tell her I am interested in women? Particularly, her.

* * *

"I know, I'm kidding. I'm sure you knew," She paused. "He is always trying to set me up with all kinds of men... and women," she laughed, once again holding her gaze with me. Her smile was drawing me.

"Women?" I asked still holding her gaze. "I thought you didn't want to go there again," I trailed off wondering if I shouldn't have mentioned her ex-girlfriend.

"Oh no, I still love hooking up with women. I find it so much more pleasing than random hook-ups with men. Sex with men is only good when you're in love with him" She grabbed a pastry and took a small bite.

"I'm starting to doubt that," I said, half under my breath.

Sarah scooted closer. "Oh no way, are you thinking of switching teams?" Her smile was wide as she sipped her drink and it dripped down her chin. I watched as it dripped down her neck and slide into her cleavage. I looked up and noticed her staring at me with a knowing smile. I felt the world melt away, she was coming on to me.

"What made you decide this?" She asked raising an eyebrow.

"I didn't, I mean I haven't 'decided' this," I was caught off guard by her question. "I was just thinking about what you said. It makes sense to me,".

* * *

"Oh, I get it, being with Mike would have me second-guessing too," she said jokingly. "Well, you're sexier than most, whatever you want you can get," She looked me up and down.

Our eyes met and once again we were staring into each other's eyes. I felt my heart skip a beat as we stayed frozen in time. I felt like she could see into my soul and I could see hers.

The waiter appeared and offered us another drink, interrupting the moment.

"Phil told me to tell the ladies the dance floor is filling up with 'hot' men," the waiter relayed Phil's message to us and Sarah immediately stood up.

"Thanks, Bill," Sarah replied then turned to me. "Let's go find us some fuck buddy's tonight," she grabbed me by the hand and ran down to the dance floor.

The music was great, and the DJ had a lot of energy. Sarah and I danced and sang our hearts out, all the while she picked out guy after guy for me. All of which I refused, which began to drive her nuts. I couldn't help but laugh at the situation. The dance floor was so loud and crowded that we couldn't talk to each other. I had to constantly figure out her hand signals and most of them indicated sex. I was having a blast until I lost Sarah and wound up dancing with strangers. One man who had been after me throughout the night approached me.

"All alone?" He leaned in and yelled in my ear. I backed away from him, smiling, and tried looking for Sarah.

"Looking for your friend?" He tried again. "She's over there," he pointed and I looked over.

I stopped in my tracks as I saw her. She was leaning in to kiss a guy on the lips. They were flirting and making out. I felt worse than my recent break-up. I didn't know why, Sarah and I were only friends, nothing more. It hit me that this was all we would ever be. I felt crushed. I stood there with my realization, not understanding why I hadn't seen it before. I had always been in love with Sarah. She's been my escape from everything in my life, I had always needed her I just didn't know how badly I needed her until right then.

I still don't know what came over me, some sort of gay epiphany but I walked through the dance floor toward her, making a beeline for Sarah. I didn't know what I was going to do when I got to her, I just knew I had to do something. I felt the adrenaline pumping through my system. As I approached her, the guy caught sight of me and pointed me out to Sarah.

As she turned around to face me I just blurted out "I think I want you,".

She grabbed me and kissed me on the lips and it felt

like fireworks on the fourth of July.

Chapter 7

The kiss was more intense than any other I had experienced. For a brief second, I thought this is it for me, for us. Without warning, she pulled away and grabbed the guy she was with, and started making out with him. I stared at them, confused. I was taken aback until she pulled me in to kiss me again, but then pulled away to kiss him and back to me again. She giggled, enjoying herself but I started to feel this going sideways. Did she not hear me say I want you?

I played along in my confusion but was glad when she broke away to go to the VIP room. I followed her to talk to her, maybe convince her to find a cab and head home but this guy was hot on our trail as well. I didn't want him to come with us, I wanted her. For the first time in my life, I felt so sure of what I wanted. I needed to find out if she wanted me the same way.

We made our way up the velvet stairs to the VIP room and she flopped down on the plush couch with her bottle of water. The random guy still in tow, I quickly grabbed the seat beside Sarah. I tried whispering in her ear that we need to talk, but I could see she was watching the guy.

"My feet are killing me in these heels," she smiled at the guy. "Will you take them off for me?"

* * *

"Anything for you ladies," He replied, eagerly. He bent down and began undoing the stiletto.

I couldn't help but roll my eyes. How was I going to get rid of him? He continued to massage her feet, while I sipped on my water watching my dreams come crashing down.

"We should get going," I said after a few intense minutes.

"What?" She shot me a look. I wasn't sure what she was thinking, did she want to stay or did she not hear what I said?

"It's 1:08 am," I said checking my watch.

She pulled me close to her, "I thought we were getting laid tonight?" Then looked over at the guy massaging her feet.

"Well, you decide what to do with him. I am not interested," I replied bluntly. She looked at me confused.

The guy was on his knees by this point, massaging up her legs and kissing between her knees and on her thighs. I could see he was hard in his pants and ready. It did nothing for me, compared to looking at her skirt riding up her legs. His hands reached farther up to her panties, wishing it was my hands. She moaned as he rubbed her over her panties.

"Oh, Matt," She moaned.

As soon as she closed her eyes enjoying his touch, I got up and left.

I began walking away to the coat room to get my jacket and head out to find a taxi. Maybe ill just head back to the hotel I had been staying at.

I exited the building into the cold night air and stood on the sidewalk looking for taxis driving by.

After a few attempts, I walked back to the building and leaned against it. I grabbed my phone to look for a ride-share app.

"Hey, do you have an extra smoke?" The man next to me asked.

"No, sorry I don't smoke," I replied, wishing I had a smoke at that moment.

"Abby!" I heard a girl yell from the door. It was Sarah.

"Where are you going? Why are you leaving? I'm coming with you!" she ran up to me in her tiny dress, coat, and purse flying behind her as she held it.

"I thought you wanted, what's his name? Matt?" I

asked.

"Matt? Oh, no that guy's name was Mitch. Matt, well Mattie, was my ex-girlfriend," She replied solemnly.

"What?" I was shocked. "Matt was your girlfriend?"

"Ex," She clarified.

"I'm so sorry I thought his name was Matt,".

"No, I'm sorry Ab, I just wanted you to have a good night," I could hear the sadness in her voice.

"I did," I replied. "We spent most of the night in a VIP room, I haven't been out in years that was amazing. I couldn't ask for better. Besides, I got to spend the whole night with you,".

We hugged each other and pulled away. I was about to ask her what she thought when I told her I want her, but the Taxi pulled up breaking my concentration.

* * *

Chapter 8

The taxi ride felt longer on the way back. My mind was racing and suddenly I lost all confidence to ask her what her thoughts were. I couldn't help but wonder if I had interpreted things wrong. I was envisioning every detail from the beginning of the night to the end, every look, every kiss, played over endlessly.

Sarah must have been reading my mind because she seemed just as nervous, looking at the window, then looking down at her fidgeting hands.

I opened my mouth to say something and she spoke at the same time. We smiled awkwardly at each other and laughed.

"You go first," I wanted to hear what was on her mind. I knew what was on my mind.

She smiled at me and blushed nervously.

"I was just going to say we should order a pizza when we get home," She said.

"Oh sure," I hid my disappointment. I thought it would be something else, maybe about us. After hearing what was on her mind I didn't feel comfortable saying what was on my mind.

"Cool, you like pep and cheese? Nothing fancy?" She asked.

"Yeah," I replied trying to sound somewhat enthusiastic. She finished the order on her phone.

"What were you going to say earlier?" She asked.

"Oh, um, the same thing ordering food," I lied.

"Oh," She said, and I couldn't help but wonder if she believed me.

I decided to remain quiet for the remainder of the ride. I felt like I had done something wrong or interpreted things wrong. I must have misinterpreted everything, I felt like a fool. Just because someone is gay doesn't mean they want you. All of this had only been in my head. I felt embarrassed.

As we walked into the building and toward the elevators, her phone rang. She checked the caller ID.

"It's Mitch," She looked surprised and excited. I felt my heart drop.

"Are you going to answer it?" I asked.

She looked up from her phone at me. "You know the code to my apartment?" She asked rhetorically and pressed answer.

"Hey sexy," she answered.

I just stared back confused as she walked off. The elevator doors opened and got in. I hit the button for her apartment floor and felt the rush of emotions hit me as the doors closed.

I entered the apartment and went straight to my room. Flashbacks of her nude body in the shower crossed my mind as I sat on my bed facing the bathroom. I felt more overwhelmed than I had ever been. I knew if Mitch came over I couldn't stay here and listen to them.

I heard the door open before I could come up with a plan.

"Ab?" She called.

I walked out of the room and she was taking off her heels. She sighed with relief as she stepped onto the plush carpet. I just felt awkward as I stared at her beautiful little painted toes.

She smiled at me and gave me a weird look I couldn't figure out. I felt like there was an elephant in the room that needed to be addressed.

"So," I started "Is Mitch coming over?"

* * *

"Oh no way," She flopped down onto her couch, then grabbed a foot to massage it. "Those heels kill me every time,".

"Oh," I felt confused.

"Why?" She asked.

"I just thought, he called right after getting home, he must be desperate," I laughed and sat down beside her. I tried to keep my eyes on her face but I wanted desperately to take over and massage her feet.

"Oh, he is," She laughed. "I just told him no," She put her foot down and smiled at me. "Mitch was someone I wanted to bring home for you,".

"Oh," I laughed. "Well, I'm glad you decided against it. But why?"

"I knew you weren't interested," she replied after a long pause. Staring into her eyes I felt like she knew what I wanted and I knew what she wanted. It's like our souls recognized one another.

My heart began to beat harder in my chest as I put two and two together. I moved closer to her on the couch. I had never been one to make the first move in any relationship, but this time was different. I grabbed her hand and held it to my cheek, staring into her eyes. She seemed surprised but knew exactly what I was doing. I kissed the back of her hand, feeling the softness of her skin. I pulled her close to me and whispered in her ear.

"What if I want you?"

And to my surprise, she whispered back, "What if I want you more?"

***

Chapter 9

I froze and second-guessed what I had heard. *Did she really say that? Did I really just say that?* A million thoughts raced through my mind. My confidence drained and my mind blanked, realizing I didn't know how to pursue this fully. I have never been with a woman and Mike always led the way in our relationship. I followed his lead, but this was different, I wanted to be with Sarah. I knew it would be different than the videos or fantasies I had.

She must have read my mind because she reached out and grabbed my hands. Without speaking, we walked hand in hand to the plush sofa. She leaned over and kissed me gently and then pulled the straps of my dress down. She leaned back and pulled one side of her dress down and then the other, exposing her breasts. She stood to remove the rest and I couldn't help but notice the way her breasts swayed with every move. Her silhouette against the moonlight was breathtaking. I was mesmerized by her naked figure.

"Your turn," She giggled standing nude, touching her breasts.

I stood up facing her and pulled my dress off. I removed the strapless bra I was wearing and let my breasts fall free, embarrassed by my small size compared to hers. I stepped out of my lacy panties. She tilted her head looking at me up and down, a small smile on her lips. Her gaze was soft until we locked eyes, and the pull was magnetic. Her lips were velvet and subtle, her sweet smell enclosing me. I felt her tongue slip through my lips to tease my tongue, the reaction was electric. I felt the electricity shoot down my body right between my legs. I was getting wetter and wetter at every touch of her tongue, squirming while we locked lips.

Tongue still down my throat I felt her hands on my breasts. She massaged them with the perfect pressure, caressing the nipples gently, my boobs had never turned me on until now. It felt good to see a woman's hand on my breasts. I reached out to feel hers, shocked by how full yet, how soft they were.

She pulled away and looked me in the eye, "I want you to feel all of me,".

I looked her up and down, pushing the hair past her shoulders, slowly moving my hand down her chest to her tiny nipples. She pushed my hand lower onto her stomach and held it there. I could feel her breath was quick. Looking me in the eye, she moved my hand slowly down her body, past her belly butt, and between her legs. As she pushed me closer to her vulva I felt how warm she was. I felt her wetness all over her labia, she pushed further and my fingers slipped into her as she moaned. I could feel myself dripping now, I wanted to see more from her, feel more from her. I pushed my fingers further and began to massage her gspot. She let go of my hand, closing her eyes as her legs trembled. I could hear the sound of her wet pussy as I wriggled my fingers inside of her. She moaned louder and then opened her eyes, grabbing my hand, and stopping me.

"Not yet, you first," She whispered.

I wanted to make her cum on my fingers but she squirmed away. I couldn't protest her because I wanted to feel her between my legs just as badly.

"You were close weren't you?" I said. She smiled at me knowingly.

She pushed me onto the couch and spread my legs wide. I felt so exposed but so turned on at the same time. I had a beautiful woman between my legs. The sensations down there had me worried I would cum as soon as she touched me.

She licked her lips as she knelt down, I felt her breath on my pussy and I was trembling. Her lips softly touched me, I felt her tongue glide gently over my pussy lips, spreading them wide open. I could tell I was leaking non-stop, all over. She pulled my hips toward her, allowing better access. I felt her tongue plunge deep into me. I moaned loudly. Her tongue pushed on the top of my vagina up to my clit. She pushed just under the clit, teasing yet the pressure was enough. I felt myself building up already. She kissed and licked me in ways I had never felt, every way was pure bliss. She knew where to go and what pressure to apply. I felt her tongue move up and down below my clit, on top of my clit, around my vagina, and back to the clit. I was trying so hard not to cum, worried I might squirt on her face. My heart was beating out of my chest and I was wriggling around trying to escape her tongue for a moment so I wouldn't explode. I knew I was already soaking her face as it was, but she was insistent she knew exactly where she needed to be to get what she wanted. Her tongue pressed directly on my clit and I exploded. I felt stream after stream pulse out of me. She didn't move her face and continued to lick, amplifying my pleasure. I let go and released all I had onto her. I no longer cared about wetting the couch or her furniture and the stream poured out of me. I had never cum so hard in my entire life, I was in pure ecstasy and everything melted away.

I looked down at her as she was covered in my juices, pouring from her mouth. It was so hot I couldn't help but lean in and make out with her. I had to taste my orgasm on her.

"I want to taste you now," I said to her as I pushed her onto the couch. I spread her legs and saw the most beautiful pussy I had ever seen, soaking wet and ready for me. I leaned in and kissed her as gently as she had for me. I tasted her sweetness in my mouth and I wanted more. I plunged my tongue between her velvet lips and wriggled upward. Pushing with my tongue up to her clit just as she had, but this time I inserted a finger into her. She moaned loudly and her legs trembled. I knew she was close already but didn't want her to cum too soon.

"Hold it," I whispered to her.

* * *

"Oh my god," she whispered back between clenched teeth. I smiled at her and dove back in. She moaned louder. My tongue plunged into her as my finger continued to apply pressure to her G-spot. I felt a slight squirt into my mouth and knew she had cum a bit trying so hard not to release. I wriggled my tongue up and on her clit applying pressure as she had with me. I felt squirt after squirt into my mouth as my finger was engulfed in her contractions. Her moans slipped out of her with every wave. I pulled out and licked my fingers, tasting both of us.

Chapter 10

I awoke the next morning to find us both in bed naked, Sarah still peacefully sleeping. The events of last night began to flood my mind and with that a whole mix of emotions. I felt embarrassed by my actions, confused about my feelings, ashamed of myself, and on top of everything, happy. I went through the night in my mind, moment by moment, remembering the magic that came from all of it. I closed my eyes and remembered her lips on mine, her soft skin, and the way she made me feel.

I heard Sarah take a big inhale and turn over to face me. Her eyes locked with mine and a small smile crept across her face. She hid her smile behind the sheets.

"Good morning beautiful," she whispered to me from behind the sheet. She lowered it and the way the morning sun crept through the curtains, highlighted the features of her face. Her hazel eyes twinkled at me.

I smiled and leaned into her, wrapping our arms around each other, our breath in unison, her heart beating with mine. I felt true bliss in those quiet moments together.

We must have fallen back to sleep because I woke to

an empty bed a few hours later. I could hear someone in the kitchen. I crawled out of bed, threw on a pair of underwear and a tank top, and headed to the main room. The smell of bacon filled the air. Sarah's back was turned as she buttered bread fresh out of the toaster. I smiled admiring her in her element. She turned to put the bread on the plate and realized I was standing there.

"Oh! Good morning," She smiled at me, I could see she was blushing.

"Good morning smells amazing in here," I replied.

"Looks amazing in here," she laughed looking me up and down, "coffee?"

"Yes please," I laughed thinking I couldn't be as beautiful as she is in the morning. "Can I just say you look amazing yourself, the morning light suits you,"?

She smiled and started blushing.

"I was going to bring you breakfast in bed, but here you are," She poured a cup of hot coffee from the carafe and handed it to me. "Sugar, milk?"

"No thanks, I take it black," I replied. She dished out the bacon, eggs, and toast with slices of tomato and avocado sprinkled with sea salt.

Handing me the plate, she sat down next to me.

"Here's to last night, the most amazing night of my life!" She laughed and took a sip of her ice water.

I couldn't help but wonder if she was nervous, or had something on her mind. My brain began coming up with why her tone had changed. Was she feeling awkward? Was she trying to find a way to tell me it was a one-off and that we should probably never do it again?

"So," She began, confirming that something was wrong. "I just wanted to, um, talk about last night,".

I put my fork down and turned toward her, nervous about what she had to say. Feeling the blissful energy sucked out of the room.

"Ya, I agree" I tried to sound confident.

"I, don't really know how to say this, but my ex-girlfriend was the only girl I had been with. I never wanted to be with a woman again," She started.

This is it, I thought, she wants to forget this and tell me it was a mistake.

Sarah dropped her eye contact and began looking at her feet, struggling to find the words.

"I need to tell you something. I need to get it off my chest. I keep debating whether to just play it cool or to tell you and see what happens," She took a deep breath. "I like you, and I know you are probably not into me, you just left a long-term relationship, but I have always had a crush on you. I couldn't hide my excitement when I found out you and Mike broke up. I don't even know why, I never in my dreams expected us to ...be together...or even have a, whatever last night was. I didn't even think you would be bisexual. It feels like I had this amazing dream but then I woke up and I need to know if it was real." She paused, "I just want to say I am so sorry for getting my emotions mixed into this,".

I smiled at the thought of her having had a crush on me all this time and I had no idea. I stood from my chair and wrapped my arms around her.

"I think I have had a crush on you since day one and didn't even know it," I began. "I was living on autopilot for so long, and with you, I feel like I've truly found myself,".

She embraced me back and we looked at each other smiling. "I was afraid you were going to tell me this was a mistake,".

"What?" She laughed brushing a tear from her eye. "Abby, I think I've been in love with you since the beginning I just didn't know how to tell you. And let me just say, knowing you were staying in my house and I couldn't have you naked in my bed, was driving me mad,".

"So," I smiled, "we were thinking the same thing

this whole time?"

"I guess so," she laid her head on my shoulder as we held each other.

"Sarah, will you be my girl?" I asked, officially.

She lifted her head off my shoulder, smiling, and gently kissed my lips.

"I will," She whispered back.

Printed in Great Britain
by Amazon

35323778R00036